To Tony
Love
Mum & Dad
have fun.
xxxx.

WISDOM
of
FROGS

Compiled by
Franchesca Ho Sang

Hylas Publishing®
129 Main Street, Ste. C
Irvington, NY 10533
www.hylaspublishing.com

Hylas Publishing
Publisher: Sean Moore
Publishing Director: Karen Prince
Art Director: Gus Yoo
Designer: La Tricia Watford
Editor: Franchesca Ho Sang
Proofreader: Ward Calhoun

ISBN: 1-59258-251-6
ISBN 13/EAN: 978-1592-58251-8

Library of Congress Cataloging–in–Publication Data available upon request.
Printed and bound in Singapore
Distributed in the United States by Publishers Group West
Distributed in Canada by Publishers Group Canada
First American Edition published in 2006

2 4 6 8 10 9 7 5 3 1

WISDOM *of* FROGS

Compiled by
Franchesca Ho Sang

www.hylaspublishing.com

"Small opportunities are often the beginning of great enterprises."

–Demosthenes

"As we **grow** as unique persons, we learn to **respect** the **uniqueness** of others."

–Robert H. Schuller

"Don't fear
change,
embrace it."

—*Anthony J. D'Angelo*

"Don't try to walk
before you crawl."
–Proverb

"There is always **a smile** behind a tear."

–Helen Luecke

"The commonest thing is **delightful**
if one only hides it."

–Oscar Wilde

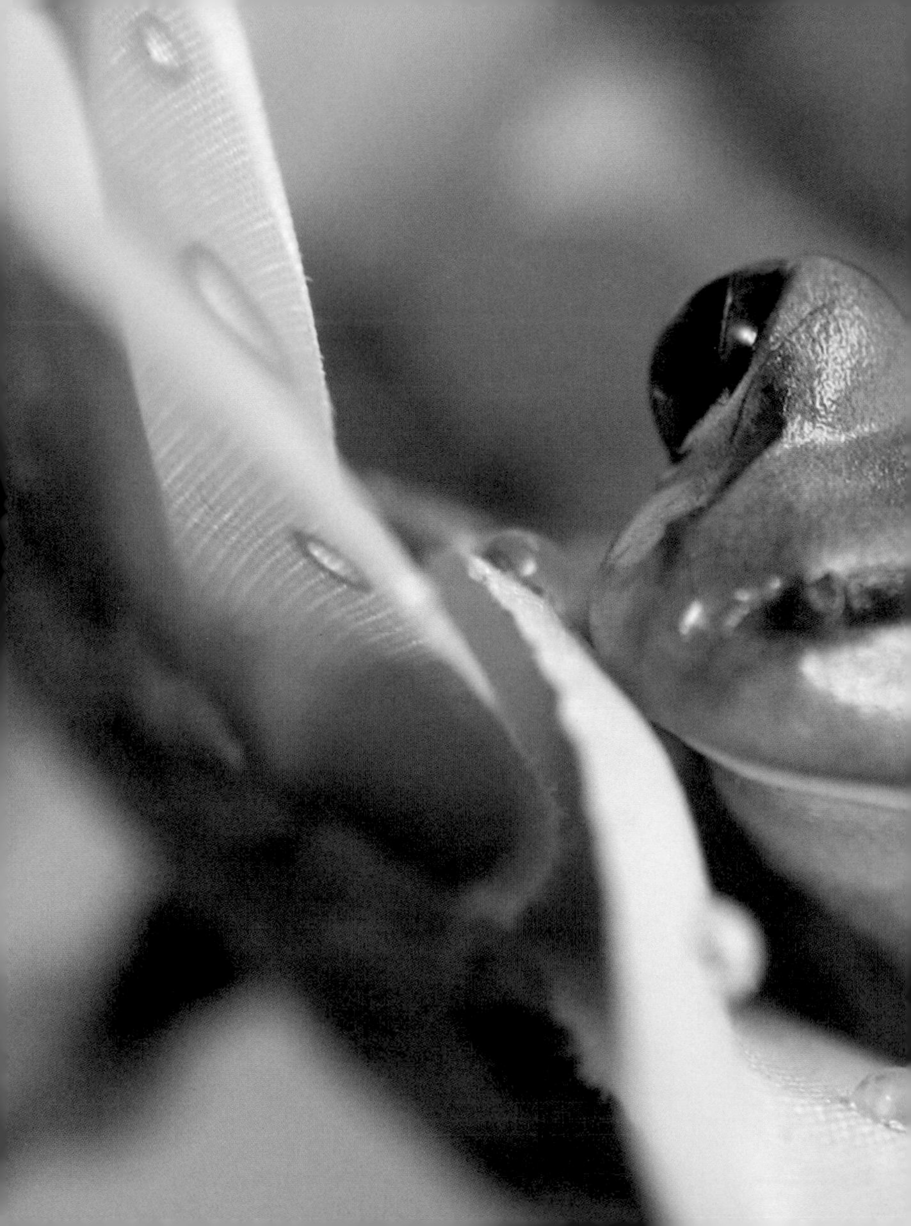

"This very **moment**
is the **seed** from which
tomorrow's **happiness grows.**"

–Margaret Lindsey

“**Stand up**
for what is right,
even if
you are standing
alone.”

–Anonymous

"In nature
we never see anything isolated,
but everything in connection
with something else,
else which is before it,
beside it, under it and over it."
–Goethe

“Let your **life** lightly dance
on the edges of Time
like dew on the tip of a leaf.”

–Rabindranath Tagore

"One mustn't **criticize** other people on grounds where he can't stand perpendicular himself."

–Mark Twain

"Do not be **too hard**, lest you be **broken**;

do not be **too soft**, lest you be **squeezed**."

–Ali ibn Abi Talib

"**Wisdom** is oft times **nearer**
when we
stoop than when we **soar.**"

–William Wordsworth

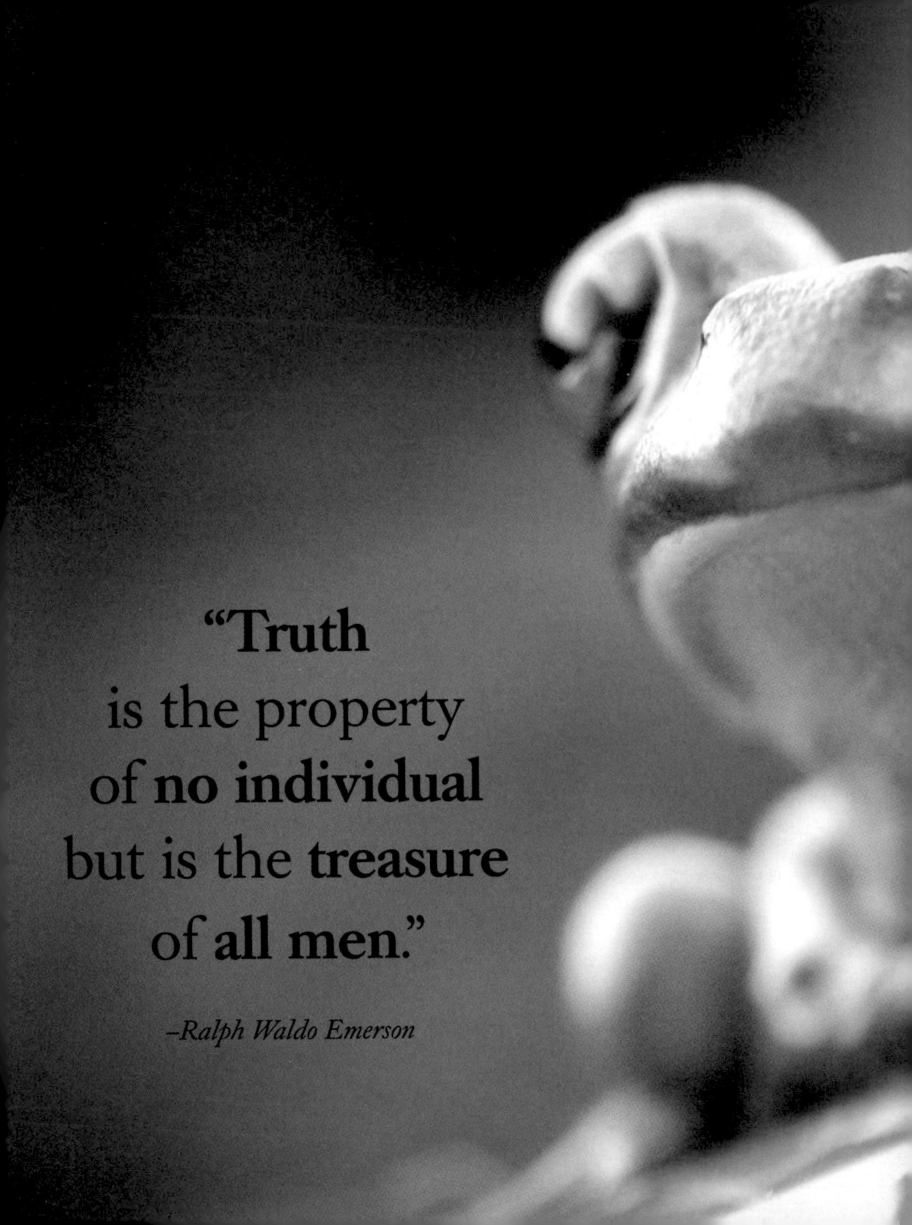
“Truth
is the property
of no individual
but is the treasure
of all men.”
–Ralph Waldo Emerson

"For here
we are **not**
afraid to **follow**
truth wherever
it may lead."

–Thomas Jefferson

"Above all, watch with **glittering eyes**
the whole world around,
because the **greatest secrets**
are always hidden
in the most **unlikely places**."

–Roald Dahl

“Without **courage,** **wisdom** bears **not** fruit.”

–Baltasar Gracian

“Keep your eyes
on the stars,
but remember
to keep your feet
on the ground.”

–Theodore Roosevelt

"Courage is the power to let go of the familiar."

–Raymond Lindquist

"You can **steer** yourself
in **any direction** you **choose.**"

–Dr. Seuss

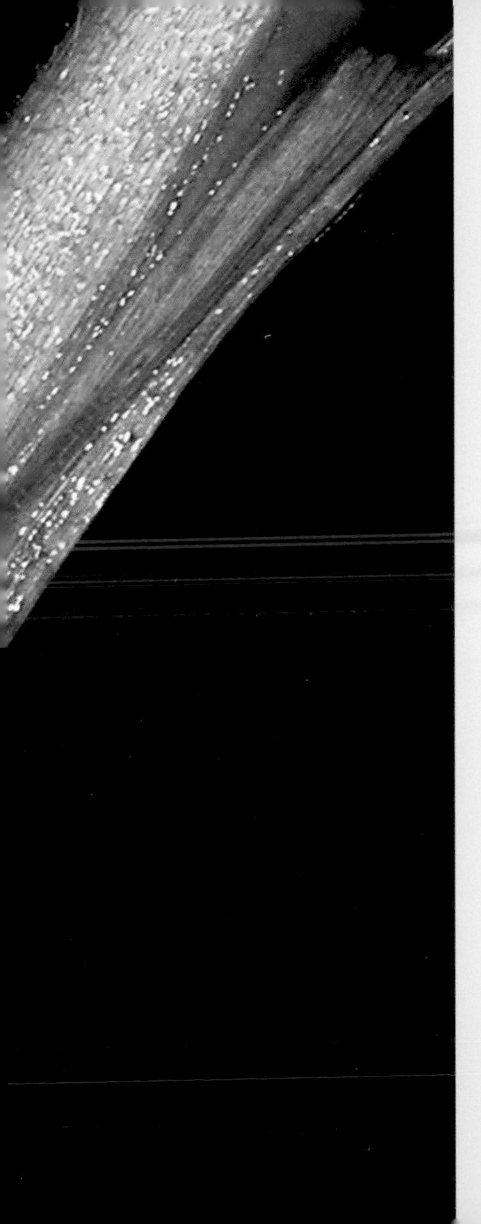

"Stop trying to
fit in
when you were
born to
stand out."

–Anonymous

"Success is a ladder
that cannot be climbed
with your hands in your pocket."

–American proverb

"Each **difficult** moment
has the **potential** to **open my eyes**
and **open my heart.**"

–Myla Kabat-Zinn

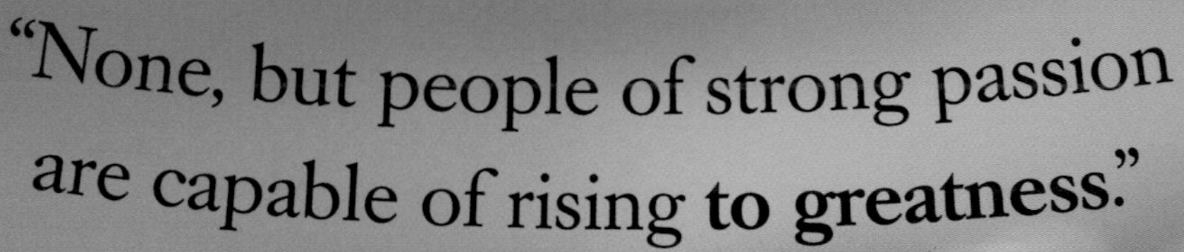

–Comte de Mirabeau

“**Genius,**
the power which dazzles human eyes
is often but
perseverance in **disguise.**”

–Mike Newlin

"Man cannot
aspire
if he looked down;
if he **rise**,
he must look up."

–Samuel Smiles

"The only people who never tumble
are those who never
mount the high wire."

–Oprah Winfrey

“When it is **darkest**, men see the **stars**.”

–Ralph Waldo Emerson

"For the wise man looks into space and he **knows** there is no **limited dimensions.**"

–Lao Tzu

"Enjoy the honey-heavy dew of slumber."

–Shakespeare

“**Fear** doesn’t exist
anywhere
except in the mind.”

–Dale Carnegie

“**Deep** into that
darkness peering,
long I stood there wondering,
fearing, Doubting,
dreaming dreams
no mortal ever dared
to **dream** before.”

–Edgar Allan Poe

"The **ultimate measure** of a man
is not where he stands
in moments of **comfort**
and **convenience**,
but where he stands
at times of **challenge** and
controversy…"

–Martin Luther King Jr.

"One sees **great things** from the valley;

only small things from the **peak.**"

–G.K. Chesterton

“He who would **search** for **pearls** **must dive** below.”

–John Dryden

"Sometimes you have to
let go to see
if there was anything
worth holding onto."

–Anonymous

“Refuse to be **average**.
Let your **heart soar**
as **high** as it will.”

–A.W. Tozer

"In order to **please others**,
we **lose** our hold
on our life's **purpose**."

–Epictetus

"**Never frown**
because you never
know who
is falling in **love**
with your **smile**."

–Anonymous

"Out of **suffering**
have emerged the **strongest** souls;
the most massive characters
are seared with scars."

–*Kahlil Gibran*

"The grass
is **always**
greener

on the
other side
of the
fence."

–*Proverb*

"To **succeed**
you need to find something to **hold on to**,
something to **motivate** you,
something to **inspire** you."

–Tony Dorsett

"There's not enough darkness

in all the world

to put out the light

of even one small candle."

–Robert Alden

"**Open** your **arms** to change,

but don't let go of your **values.**"

–Dalai Lama

"A **hero** is
one who knows how to **hang on**
one minute longer."

–Norwegian proverb

"Better a **diamond** with a flaw than a pebble without."

–Confucious

"Tough times never last, but tough people do."

–Robert H. Schuller

"When **fortune** calls,

offer her a chair."

–Yiddish proverb

“Conceit may **puff** a man **up**, but never prop him up.”

–John Ruskin

"Some people
make things happen,
some
watch things happen,
while others wonder
what has happened."
–Proverb

"When
you want to marry a
PRINCE
you will have to kiss many frogs."

-Dutch proverb

"A sense of **curiosity** is nature's original school of **education**."

–Smiley Blarton

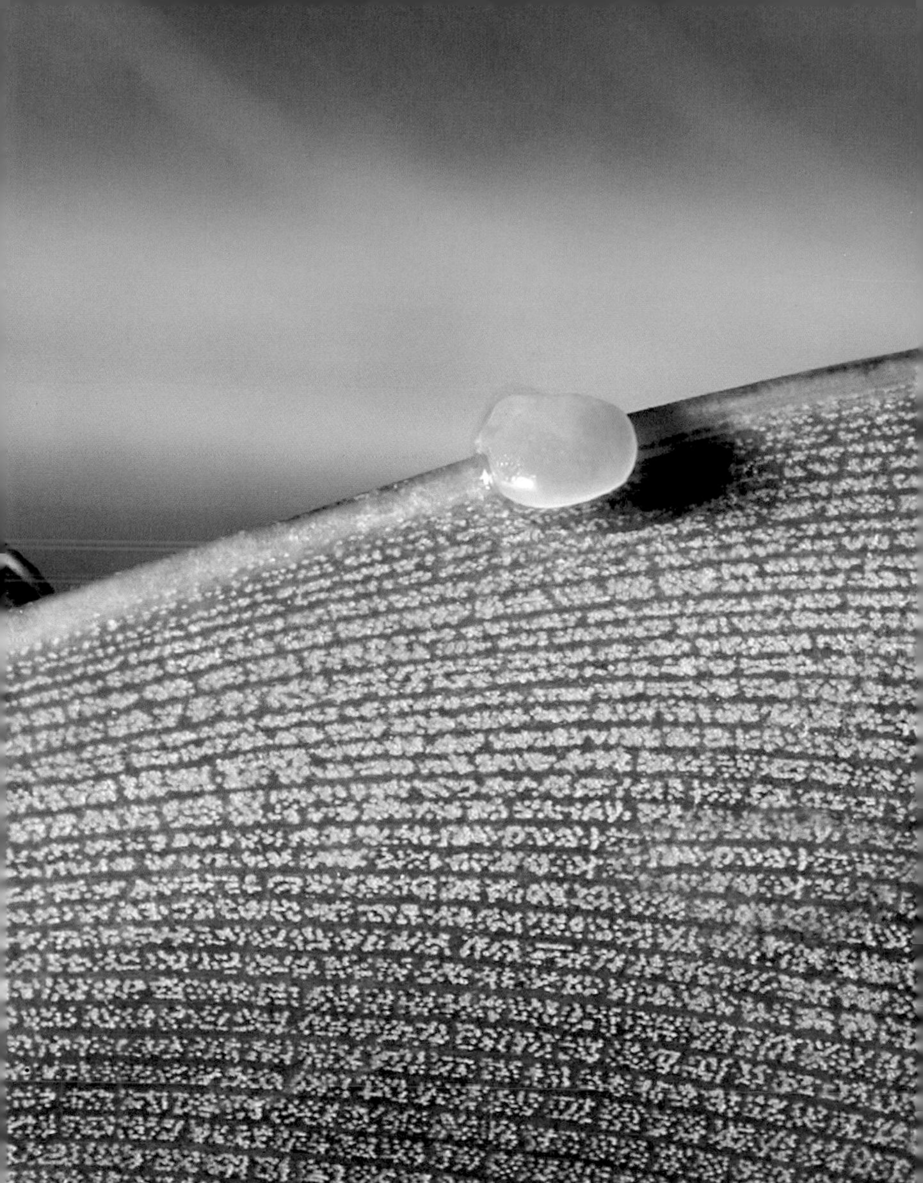

“The way to **see by Faith** is to shut the **Eye of Reason.**”

–Benjamin Franklin

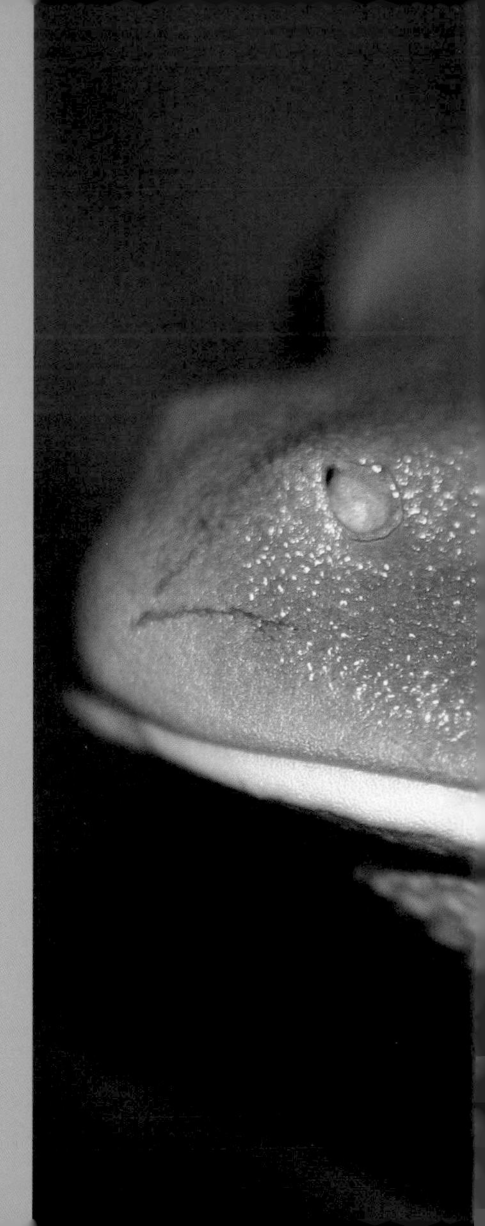

"**Seeking** and searching, I have found my **own home**, deep within my **own being**."

–Sri Guru Granth Sahib

"It's not easy
being GREEN."

–Kermit the Frog

"Our way
is **not soft grass,**
it's a mountain
path with lots of
rocks. But it goes
upwards, forward,
toward the **sun.**"

–Dr. Ruth Westheimer

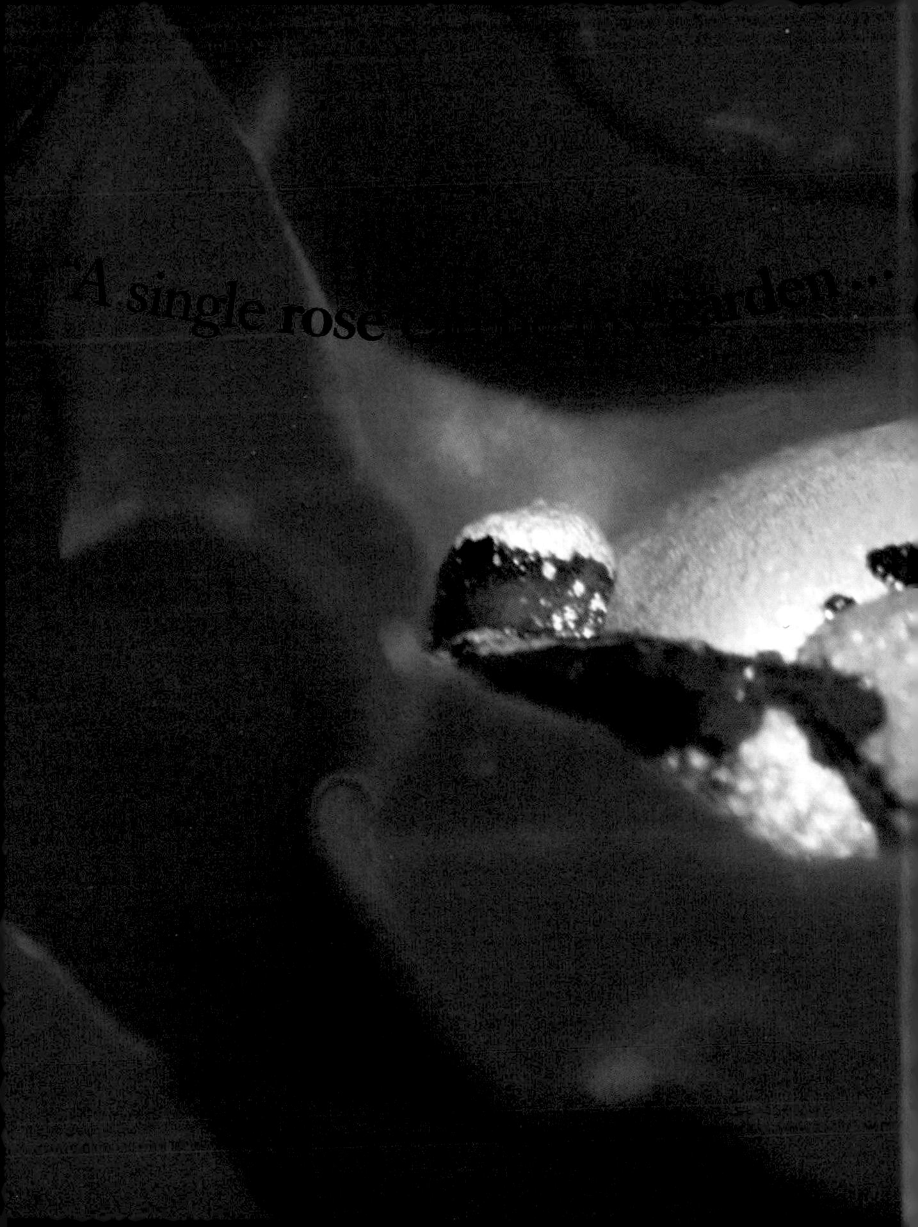

"A single rose [illegible] arden…

a single friend, my world.”

PICTURE CREDITS

Cover: Shutterstock
Front Endpaper: Indexopen
Page iv: Shutterstock
Page 8: Shutterstock
Page 11: Photos.com
Page 12: Photos.com
Page 14: Shutterstock
Page 16: Istockphoto
Page 18: Istockphoto
Page 20: Shutterstock
Page 22: Istockphoto
Page 24: Shutterstock
Page 27: Shutterstock
Page 28: Indexopen
Page 30: Shutterstock
Page 32: Photos.com
Page 34: Shutterstock
Page 36: Shutterstock
Page 38: Shutterstock
Page 41: Istockphoto
Page 42: Shutterstock
Page 44: Istockphoto
Page 46: Shutterstock
Page 48: Shutterstock
Page 50: Istockphoto
Page 52: Istocphoto
Page 54: Istockphoto
Page 56: Istockphoto
Page 59: Shutterstock
Page 60: Istockphoto
Page 62: Shutterstock
Page 65: Istockphoto
Page 68: Istockphoto
Page 71: Shutterstock
Page 72: Indexopen
Page 74: Shutterstock
Page 76: Istockphoto
Page 77: Istockphoto
Page 78: Shutterstock
Page 80: Shutterstock
Page 83: Indexopen
Page 84: Shutterstock
Page 86: Shutterstock
Page 88: Istockphoto
Page 90: Istockphoto
Page 93: Istockphoto
Page 94: Indexopen
Page 96: Istockphoto
Page 98: Shutterstock
Page 100: Shutterstock
Page 102: Indexopen
Page 104: Photos.com
Page 106: Istockphoto
Page 108: Shutterstock
Page 110: Istockphoto
Page 113: Shutterstock
Page 114: Istockphoto
Page 116: Shutterstock
Page 118: Istockphoto
Page 120: Indexopen
Page 123: Shutterstock
Back Endpaper: Indexopen